I
Believe
IN
UNICORNS

I Believe in Unicorns

ADAM JOHN MUNTHE

ELIZABETH FALCONER

CHATTO & WINDUS · LONDON

Once there was a Unicorn.
He was born one crisp
winter's night,
leaping from
a fiery
volcano.

On the same night, in the far north,
a little boy, with blue slanting eyes,
leapt from his mother
and was tossed into this world.
His father, who fished
in the great waters off the coast,
was glad. He had a son now
who one day would help
him pull in the nets.

The Unicorn grew lonely.
He had no family except the wind,
no brothers or sisters except
the bright stars, no friends except for
the wild creatures,
but they disdained him,
for he was not like them.

Raif was lonely too.
His father was often away fishing, and his
mother worked all day in the fields, so Raif played alone
with only birdsong for company. He listened to the falcon's
kreen, and watched silently as the arctic fox and her cubs
slipped from their lair.

One day he found a
dried-out tree root.
It was smooth and
beautiful to him,
like a Unicorn.
He kept it, and at night
he dreamt of being small
enough to gallop through
his bedroom window,
and make a journey
to the stars.

The Unicorn travelled the world.
His hooves beat out magical rimes
on a thousand roof-tops.
The music of his heels
touched echoes in
a million hearts,
but men did
not recognise
him, nor
the songs
which he
sang.
But Raif
heard his roar.

Raif threw open his window. He gazed at the stars.
"Father," he asked, "does the Unicorn live in the sky?"
"No," his father replied, closing the window, "it's only a
traveller's tale." Raif sighed as he got into bed, but in his
dreams he rode his magic Unicorn all over the skies. The
Unicorn drew near on silent feet and stared longingly at
the sleeping boy, and in the morning Raif saw where
his breath had frozen on the window-pane.

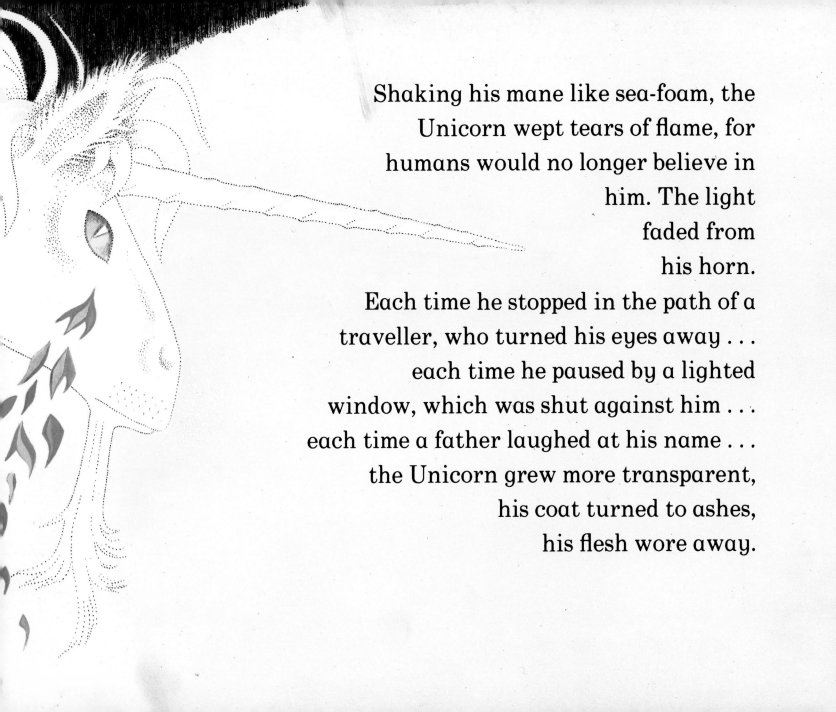

Shaking his mane like sea-foam, the
Unicorn wept tears of flame, for
humans would no longer believe in
him. The light
faded from
his horn.
Each time he stopped in the path of a
traveller, who turned his eyes away . . .
each time he paused by a lighted
window, which was shut against him . . .
each time a father laughed at his name . . .
the Unicorn grew more transparent,
his coat turned to ashes,
his flesh wore away.

One day Raif's mother fell ill and had to stay in bed.
Raif was not big enough to help her in the fields.
He could not do her work.
Her eyes and hungry cheeks made him tremble.
Raif took her cold hand in his, and told her
about his dreams of the wonderful Unicorn.
"I've seen him," he said, "and heard him sing,
and there's magic in him that makes people
better, if only they believe in him
hard enough."
There were tears in his mother's eyes
as she shook her head, but she
smiled at her son, and kissed him.

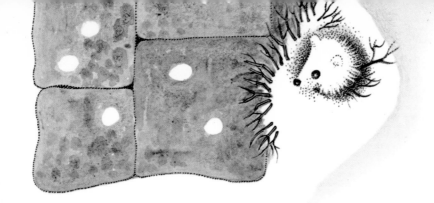

That night Raif stared out of the window.

He felt very sleepy.

At last a whisper crept from his throat:

"Doesn't the Unicorn live any more?

Doesn't he?"

His heart grew heavier, for the wind
seemed to blow the words back in his face.

It was close to dawn. The Unicorn,
with weariness deep in his bones, paused for
breath on an ice-floe travelling to the ocean.
A light shone from a lonely cabin, and the Unicorn
felt faintly the pull of a human sadness. He saw a
small boy wandering towards the dark woods.
Quietly he approached.

Closer came the Unicorn, until the warm breath from his nostrils touched Raif's cheek. Raif looked up but saw nothing. Suddenly he cried: "They're wrong! They're wrong! I dreamed of him, and his songs put the leap into the lame!" He took out his knife and began to carve the letters on the trunk of a tree, whispering the words softly to himself as he worked:

"I BELIEVE IN UNICORNS!"

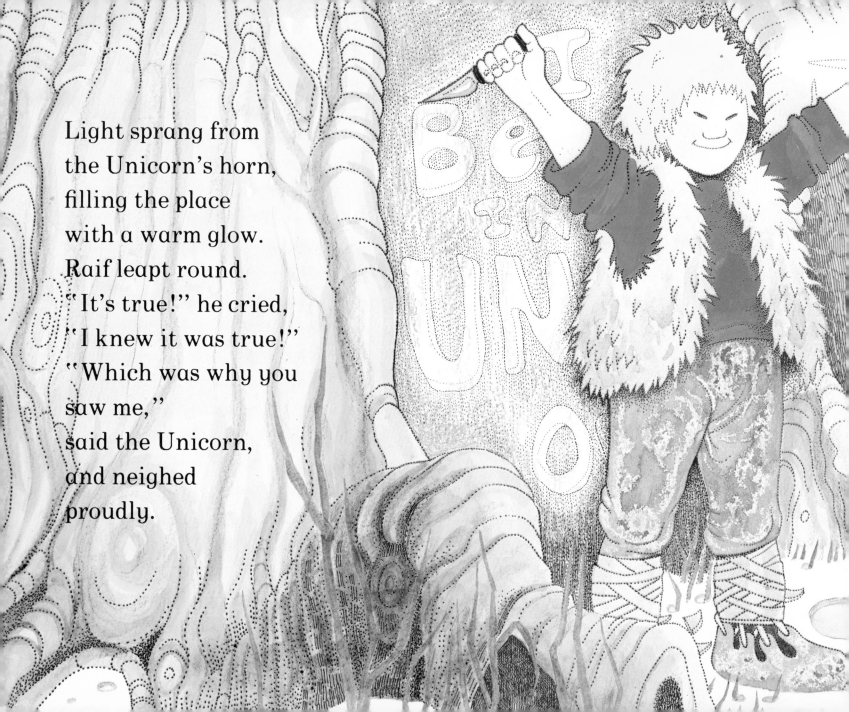

Light sprang from
the Unicorn's horn,
filling the place
with a warm glow.
Raif leapt round.
"It's true!" he cried,
"I knew it was true!"
"Which was why you
saw me,"
said the Unicorn,
and neighed
proudly.

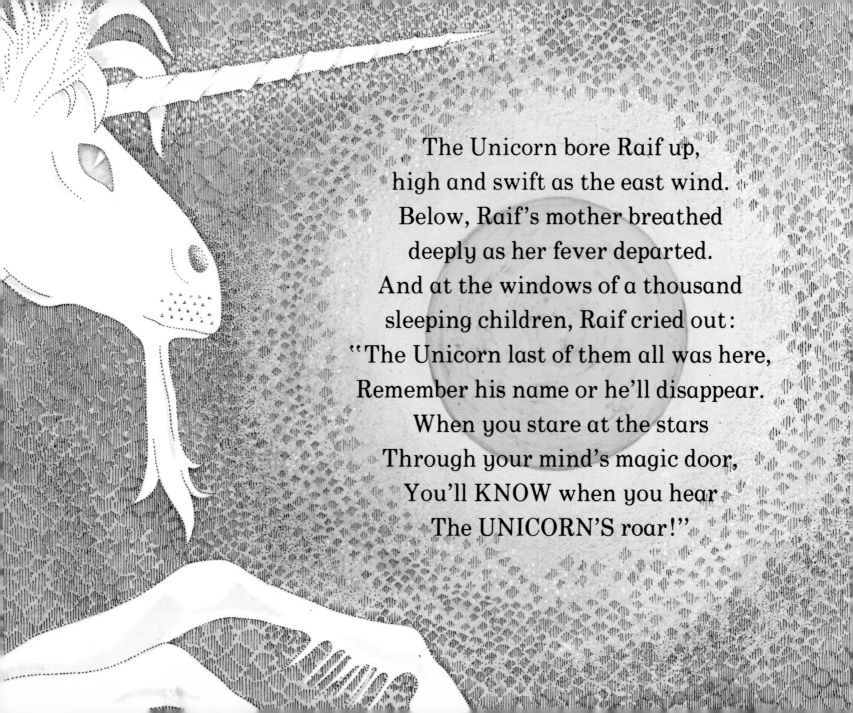

The Unicorn bore Raif up,
high and swift as the east wind.
Below, Raif's mother breathed
deeply as her fever departed.
And at the windows of a thousand
sleeping children, Raif cried out:
"The Unicorn last of them all was here,
Remember his name or he'll disappear.
When you stare at the stars
Through your mind's magic door,
You'll KNOW when you hear
The UNICORN'S roar!"

Published by Chatto & Windus Ltd
40 William IV Street, London WC2N 4DF

*

Clarke, Irwin & Co. Ltd., Toronto

Text (C) Adam John Munthe 1979
Illustrations (C) Elizabeth Falconer 1979
First edition 1979

Munthe, Adam John
I believe in unicorns
I. Title II. Falconer, Elizabeth
823'.9'1F PZ7.M/
ISBN 0-7011-2437-7

Printed and bound in Great Britain by
William Clowes & Sons, Limited
London, Beccles and Colchester